Jaws

PETER BENCHLEY

Level 2

Retold by Keiran McGovern
Series Editors: Andy Hopkins and Jocelyn Potter

Pearson Education Limited
Edinburgh Gate, Harlow,
Essex CM20 2JE, England
and Associated Companies throughout the world.

ISBN: 978-1-4058-6952-2

First published in Great Britain by André Deutsch Ltd 1974
This adaptation first published by Penguin Books 1998
Published by Addison Wesley Longman Ltd and Penguin Books Ltd 1998
This edition first published 2008

3 5 7 9 10 8 6 4 2

Typeset by Graphicraft Ltd, Hong Kong
Set in 11/14pt Bembo
Printed in China
SWTC/02

Published by Pearson Education Ltd in association with
Penguin Books Ltd, both companies being subsidiaries of Pearson Plc

Contents

Introduction

The boy stopped, and the shark swam below him. Then it turned again. The shark swam up fast. Its mouth opened . . .

Amity is a quiet town near New York. Nothing happens there.

One night a young woman goes for a swim in the sea. It's a warm night in June. She doesn't come back. The next morning the police find her body on the beach.

Brody is a good policeman. He thinks there's a shark near Amity. Young Matt Hooper says it's a Great White Shark, a man-eater.

Brody tries to close the beaches, but the important people in Amity don't listen to him. It's holiday time. People from New York come to Amity at holiday time, and they bring money to the town.

Then, on a sunny afternoon, a young boy goes into the sea . . .

Peter Benchley was born in New York City in 1940. In the 1960s he had many different jobs. He worked for *The Washington Post* newspaper and for *Newsweek* magazine. He worked for President Johnson at the White House. And he worked in television.

In 1964 he read a story in a newspaper about a fisherman. The fisherman caught a Great White shark in the sea near New York. Ten years later, Peter remembered the story and he wrote *Jaws*. Many people bought the book.

In 1975, Steven Spielberg made an exciting film from the story. People round the world saw the film. Peter Benchley helped to write the story for the film. He is in the film, too. He is the man from the newspaper on the beach.

Peter Benchley wrote many more books. The most famous are *The Deep* (1976) and *The Island* (1979). Twenty years later, he wrote about sharks again in *White Shark* (1994). He died in 2006.

PART ONE

Chapter 1 Night Swim

The shark moved through the night water without a sound. It swam towards the shore, with its eyes and mouth open.

Between the sea and the shore was a long beach. Behind that beach there was a house, with lights in its windows.

The front door of the house opened, and a man and woman came out. They stood for a short time and looked at the sea. Then they ran down to the beach.

The man sat down and closed his eyes. The woman smiled at him and said, 'Do you want to go for a swim?'

'You go on. I'll wait for you here.'

She began walking out towards the sea. The water came up round her feet. It was a warm June night, but the water felt cold.

The woman called back. 'Come and have a swim with me!' But there was no answer from the man.

She ran into the sea, and soon the water was up to her head. She began to swim.

The shark was a hundred metres from the beach. It could not see the woman – it could not see anything in the dark water – but it felt the sea move. It turned towards the shore.

The woman swam away from the beach. After about a hundred metres she began to feel tired and stopped for a short time. Then she turned and began swimming back to the shore.

The shark moved closer to the woman. For the first time she felt afraid, but she did not know why. She looked up and saw the lights in the house. She was about seventy metres from the shore. She began to swim faster.

The shark was now above the water, about fifteen metres from the woman. Suddenly it dropped down to the left.

The woman felt something hit her right leg. She put her hand into the water and tried to find her foot. Then she cried out.

The shark turned and then turned again. This time it attacked the woman from below. It swam up fast and pushed her out of the water.

The shark carried the woman away in its mouth. It came up out of the water and then went under again. A short time later it began swimming away from the shore.

♦

The woman felt something hit her right leg. She put her hand into the water and tried to find her foot. Then she cried out.

The man opened his eyes. It was dark and he felt cold. He stood up and began to dress. It was then he saw the woman's shoes on the beach. He picked up the shoes and walked back to the house.

The door to the woman's room was open, and the light was on. But she was not there.

There were two more rooms in the house. The man opened the door of the first bedroom and went across to the bed.

'Jack.'

The man in the bed opened his eyes. 'What?'

'It's me. Tom. I think there's something wrong. Where's Chrissie?'

'I thought she was with you.'

'No, she isn't. I can't find her. She's not in the house and she's not on the beach.'

Jack sat up and turned on a light. He looked at his watch. It was five in the morning. 'I'll phone the police,' he said.

Chapter 2 Body on the Beach

'Mr Brody, this is Hendricks. We've got a problem. We had a call from a house on Old Mill Road a few minutes ago. A girl went out on the beach there last night and she didn't come back. They –'

'What time is it?'

'Five-thirty. Sorry!'

'No, you were right to call. Tell me everything you know.'

It was nearly six-thirty when Brody drove his police car along Old Mill Road. He looked all along the beach but did not see anything unusual. At eight o'clock Hendricks arrived, and the two policemen called at Jack Foote's house.

A young man opened the door. 'I'm Tom Cassidy,' he said. 'Did you find her?'

'No, Mr Cassidy, we didn't find her,' said Brody. 'We're going to look on the beach now.'

'I want to come, too,' said Cassidy.

The three men walked down to the beach. 'I went to sleep here,' said Cassidy. 'And I found the shoes here.'

Brody looked up and down the beach. 'Let's walk,' he said. 'Come with me, Mr Cassidy. Leonard, can you walk back towards Mr Foote's house?'

Hendricks took his shoes off and began to walk. The beach felt cold and wet under his feet. After about fifteen minutes he turned and looked back. Brody and Cassidy were now a half kilometre down the beach so he began to walk towards them.

Suddenly Hendricks saw something in front of him. He walked quickly towards it and then stopped. For a short time he did not move. Then he cried out.

In front of him was a woman's head and some of her arm.

♦

Brody and Cassidy ran down the beach to Hendricks. Brody arrived first. He looked down and saw the woman. Then he closed his eyes. 'Mr Cassidy, is this her?'

Cassidy was very afraid. His eyes moved from Hendricks to Brody. Then he looked down.

'Oh no!' he cried, and he put his hand to his mouth.

'Is it her?'

He turned away. 'Yes,' he said. 'What happened?'

'I don't know,' said Brody. 'But I think a shark attacked her.'

♦

That afternoon Brody met his friend Harry Meadows. Harry wrote for the town's newspaper, *The Amity Leader*.

'I think it was a shark attack,' said Brody.

'You're right,' said Meadows. 'This afternoon I talked to a

young man called Matt Hooper. He knows everything about sharks.'

'What did he say?'

'He thinks it's a Great White Shark. They call the Great White the "man-eater". Other sharks don't usually attack people.'

'Does he think it will attack again?'

'No. Hooper thinks this was an accident. He thinks the shark is now far away.' Meadows looked at Brody. 'It's not going to happen again,' he said. 'And I'm not going to write about the accident in *The Amity Leader*.'

'But it's a big story for your newspaper.'

'I know, Martin. But it's summer and this town must have visitors in the summer. People are afraid of sharks.'

'That's true, Harry,' said Brody. 'But I want to close the beaches for one or two days. And I want you to write the story.'

Meadows sat back in his chair. 'I can't do that, Harry,' he said. 'My bosses don't want me to. And I don't want to lose my job.'

♦

Ten minutes later, Lawrence P. Vaughan came into Brody's office.

Larry Vaughan was an old friend of Brody's. He bought and sold houses, and made a lot of money. He was one of the most important people in the town.

Vaughan sat down. 'Please don't close the beaches,' he said. 'It will soon be the Fourth of July. That's our best weekend every summer.'

'I don't want any more shark attacks,' said Brody.

'There won't be any more shark attacks! But people will read about sharks in Amity, and they won't come here!'

Brody looked at his old friend. He liked Larry, but he did not see him much these days. 'OK,' he said. 'I don't like it, but I won't close the beaches.'

Vaughan smiled for the first time. 'Thanks, Martin,' he said.

His wife, Ellen, was in the living-room. He went and sat next to her.

Brody arrived home two or three minutes before five. His wife, Ellen, was in the living-room.

'Hello,' she said. 'What's wrong? Did something happen today?'

He went and sat next to her.

'A shark killed a girl near Old Mill Beach.'

She looked at him. 'What are you going to do?'

'Nothing. Larry Vaughan doesn't want me to do anything. He wants the beaches to stay open.'

Chapter 3 No Time to Cry

The next few days were hot, and summer visitors from New York began arriving in Amity.

Sunday was the twentieth of June. By twelve in the afternoon there were many people on Old Mill Beach. Children played near the water.

A boy of six walked up the beach. He sat down next to his mother.

'Can I go swimming?' he asked.

His mother turned to look at him. 'No. It's too cold.'

'Can I go out on my boat? I won't go far. And I won't go swimming. I'll just sit on my boat.'

His mother sat up. She looked up and down the beach. Fifty metres away a man stood in the water. He had a child on his back.

'Yes. But don't go too far out. And don't swim.'

'OK,' he said. He pulled the little boat out into the water and climbed on to it.

The shark swam under the water. It was sixty metres from the shore.

The boy sat on his boat and looked back towards the beach. His mother was about fifty metres away. He put his feet into the water and kicked towards the shore.

The shark saw nothing, but it felt the sea move. It knew there was something near, and began to swim up towards the surface. It moved slowly first, then faster.

The boy stopped, and the shark swam below him. Then it turned again.

The shark swam up fast. Its mouth opened.

The boy could not cry out – he had no time. The shark's head hit the boat and pushed it out of the water. Nearly half of the fish – with the boy and most of the boat in its mouth – came above the surface. Its jaws closed together and cut off the boy's legs. They dropped slowly down into the water.

On the beach the man with the child turned to his son and pointed at the sea. 'Did you see that?'

'What, Daddy?' His child looked up at him.

People were running away from the sea.

'Out there! A shark or something! Something very big!'

The boy's mother opened her eyes. She looked over at the man, and saw him point at the water. People were running away from the sea.

She sat up. Suddenly she remembered. 'Alex,' she said.

♦

The phone rang. Brody got up from his lunch and answered it. When he came back he looked afraid and angry.

'What is it?' asked Ellen.

'A shark attack. On a child.'

'Oh no!' And you didn't close the beaches . . .' She stopped.

'Yes, I know,' he said. 'I didn't do my job.'

Twenty minutes later Brody arrived at the police station. The boy's mother was in the office.

'I'm sorry,' said Brody.

The woman began to cry.

Suddenly the door opened and Hendricks ran into the room. 'Shark attack!' he cried.

'We know, Leonard,' said Brody. 'This is the boy's mother.'

'Boy?' said Hendricks. 'What boy? This was a man, an old man. Five minutes ago.'

◆

On Monday morning, Brody arrived at the police station soon after seven. He went into his office and found a newspaper on his desk. On the front of the newspaper it said, *SHARK ATTACK KILLS TWO IN AMITY*.

Brody sat down and began to read the story.

'Is that from New York?'

Brody looked up and saw Meadows at the door. 'Yes. Did you write about it, too?'

'I did,' said Meadows. 'And I spoke to Matt Hooper last night.'

'Does he think that one fish is doing all this?'

'He doesn't know, but he thinks it is. He thinks it's a Great White.'

'I do, too. I don't know a white shark from a green shark. But I think it's one fish. Can we do anything . . . ?'

'Yes, there's one thing,' said Meadows. 'We can put food in the water for the shark. That'll bring him to us.'

'But then what do we do?'

'We catch him. With a harpoon.'

'Harry, I don't have a police boat! And I don't have harpoons.'

'There are fishermen here. They have . . .' A noise outside the office stopped Meadows.

Suddenly the door opened, and a woman ran into the room with a newspaper in her hand. It was the mother of Alex Kintner.

Hendricks came up behind her and said, 'I'm sorry, Mr Brody, I tried to stop her.'

'That's OK, Leonard,' said Brody. 'Come in, Mrs Kintner.'

She walked up to Brody.

'What can I do . . . ?'

The woman hit him in the face with the newspaper. Brody jumped back. The newspaper fell to the floor. 'You *knew* it was dangerous!' she cried. 'You *knew* that the shark killed somebody on Thursday. But you didn't *do* anything.'

Brody did not answer for a second. Then he said, 'Yes, it's true, but it's – Mrs Kintner . . .'

The woman looked into Brody's eyes and began to cry. 'You killed Alex!' she said. 'Why?'

'It's . . .' Brody did not have the words. 'It's a long story,' he said.

Chapter 4 *Flicka*

Brody sat on the beach and looked at the sea.

'Hello, Mr Brody,' Hendricks said. He walked up to Brody. 'What are you doing here?'

'Ben Gardner went out there this morning. He's looking for the shark. But I can't see him on his boat.'

'Was there anybody with him?'

'I don't know.'

'Do you want to go and see? It'll be light for two more hours. I can get a fast boat.'

Brody felt afraid. He was a very bad swimmer. 'OK,' he said. 'You get the boat. I'll call his wife.'

Twenty minutes later Brody climbed into the Hendricks' boat.

'What did she say?' asked Hendricks.

'Nothing. She called him on his radio, but there was no answer. Perhaps he turned it off.'

'And there was nobody with him?'

'No.'

'I don't understand,' said Hendricks. 'Why did he turn his radio off? People don't usually do that.'

Hendricks started the boat, and they moved out to sea. Gardner's boat was more than a kilometre from the shore. As they got nearer, Brody read its name: *Flicka*.

When they were fifty metres from the *Flicka*, Hendricks slowed the boat down.

Brody stood up and called out, 'Ben!' There was no answer.

The two men climbed on to the fishing boat. 'Are you here, Ben?' Again, there was no answer.

There was a sudden noise and Brody jumped. It was from the radio.

Brody looked at Hendricks. 'He didn't turn off his radio . . .'

'I don't understand it, Mr Brody. Did Ben fall overboard? But he's not in the water – and he swims very well.'

Brody looked down into the water and saw four holes in the boat. 'Look at these, Leonard. Can you see what made them?'

Hendricks went down into the sea and looked at the holes. After a few seconds he looked up and said, 'Have you got a knife?'

Brody gave Hendricks a knife. 'What can you see?' he asked.

'I don't know. Something white in one of the holes.'

Hendricks put his head back down into the water. After a short time, he came up and said, 'OK. I've got it.'

Brody helped Hendricks back on to the boat and Hendricks dropped something big and white into Brody's hand.

'It's a tooth!' said Hendricks. 'Oh no! Do you think the shark got Ben?'

Brody did not answer. He looked at the tooth again. Then he put it in his bag. 'We can't do anything here now,' he said.

♦

It was nearly dark when they got back. Harry Meadows met them. He had a young man with him.

'This is Matt Hooper, Martin. What did you find out there?'

Brody told them about the boat. Then he took out the tooth and handed it to Hooper.

'What is it Matt?' said Meadows.

Hooper looked at the tooth. 'It's from a very big Great White Shark.'

'What do you think happened?'

'I think this fish killed Mr Gardner.'

'How?' said Brody.

'Perhaps he fell overboard. Perhaps the fish pulled him over.'

'What about the tooth in the boat?'

'The fish attacked the boat.'

'What for?'

'Sharks are not very clever, Mr Brody. They try to eat everything.'

'But a boat . . . !'

'A shark doesn't think. To him it wasn't a boat. It was something big in the water. Remember that sharks are afraid of nothing in the sea. They attack anything.'

'And why is he staying around here for so long?'

'I don't know. It's unusual, but sharks *are* unusual. We don't understand much about them. But I can try and find this shark. Can I have a boat?'

'Yes, I'm sorry to say,' said Brody. 'Ben Gardner's. We'll get you out to it tomorrow. Do you think you can catch that fish?'

'I'm not going to catch it.'

'Then what are you going to do?'

'I don't know. I'll see.'

Brody looked into Hooper's eyes and said, 'I want somebody to kill that fish.'

Hooper laughed. 'Who are you going to get to do the job?'

'There's a fisherman called Quint,' said Meadows. 'But I don't know much about him. He works somewhere near Promised Land Beach.'

'No, you listen, Larry. I listened to you before, and two people died.'

Hooper said, 'Look, Mr Brody, this is only a shark!'

Brody began to feel angry. Hooper did not understand!

The next day Larry Vaughan met Brody and Hooper. 'Hello, Martin. I heard about Ben Gardner. What are you going to *do*?'

'We closed the beaches down.'

'I know that! Nobody is coming to Amity now.'

'So what do you want *me* to do?' said Brody.

'I thought . . . Can we open the beaches for the Fourth of July weekend?'

'No, we cannot.'

'Now listen . . .'

'No, you listen, Larry. I listened to you before, and two people died. We're going to catch that fish. Then we'll open the beaches.'

'But this town is dying!'

'I know, Larry,' said Brody. 'But we can do nothing about it.'

Chapter 5 Shark!

The next weekend Amity was very quiet. The beaches did not open.

Hooper went up and down the shore in Ben Gardner's boat. 'I don't think that shark is here,' he told Brody on Sunday night. 'There are other fish near the beaches. And other fish don't stay in the water near Great White Sharks.'

'Perhaps you are right,' said Brody. 'But I want the beaches to stay closed.'

On Thursday morning Larry Vaughan called Brody into his office. Hooper was there, and there were some other important men from the town.

Everybody sat around a table. Then Vaughan said, 'Martin, we want you to open the beaches. The town is dying. People are losing their jobs.'

'And what do we do about the shark?' said Brody.

Vaughan said, 'Mr Hooper will tell us about that.'

'I don't think the shark will come back,' said Hooper.

'I'm sorry,' said Brody. 'I'm not opening the beaches.'

Larry Vaughan was very angry. 'The people of this town gave you your job. You work for us.'

Brody said, 'You can have my job any time you want it.'

The phone rang on Vaughan's desk. He looked very angry but he picked it up. 'It's for you, Martin,' he said.

Brody went outside to take the call. It was from Harry Meadows.

'What's happening?' said Harry.

'They want me to open the beaches,' said Brody. 'What shall I do, Harry?'

'Open them.'

'But why!'

'I think Hooper is right. And Vaughan is going to open the beaches. You can't stop him.'

'OK,' said Brody. 'I'll think about it. Thanks for the call.' He put down the phone and went back into Vaughan's office.

Brody looked at his old friend. 'I'll open the beaches,' he said.

'Thanks, Martin.'

'I'm not finished. I'll open the beaches, but Hooper will go up and down in the boat. I want everybody to know the danger.'

'You can't do that!' Vaughan said.

'I can do it, Larry, and I will.'

♦

On Saturday morning Brody stood on the Scotch Road Beach.

About a kilometre out to sea Hooper was in Ben Gardner's old boat. Brody watched it move slowly to the east.

Brody took out his radio and said, 'Hooper, this is Brody. Is there anything out there?' There was no answer. 'Hooper, this is Brody. Can you hear me?'

A short time later Hooper answered. 'Sorry,' he said. 'I thought I saw something. The light is very strong out here.'

It was a sunny day. Most of the people on the beach were young. Nobody was in the sea.

A man and woman came over to Brody. They were very fat. Behind them were two children.

'Can I help you?' Brody said.

'Is this the beach with the shark?' said the man. 'I saw it on TV.'

'There *was* a shark here,' said Brody. 'But it isn't here now. And with any luck, it won't come back.'

The family went away. They were not happy. Brody looked at his watch. It was 12.15.

By 2.30 there were not many people on the beach. Brody walked down towards the water. A boy walked past.

'What are you doing?' said Brody to the boy.

'I'm going swimming.'

'Don't stay in too long.'

'I won't.' The boy ran into the water and began to swim. Brody watched him swim out a hundred metres.

Suddenly the *Flicka* began to move faster. Brody put his radio to his mouth and said, 'Can you see something, Hooper?'

The boat slowed and then stopped. Another of Brody's policemen heard him speak. 'What's happening?' he asked.

'I don't know,' said Brody. Again he said into the radio, 'Can you see anything, Hooper?'

'Yes. I can see something,' Hooper answered.

'What is it?'

'I don't know . . . Perhaps my eyes are tired.'

'There's a boy swimming out there,' said Brody.

'Where?' said Hooper.

'About fifty metres out. I'll tell him to come in.' Brody turned the radio off. Then he put his hands to his mouth and called out, 'Come in!'

The boy did not hear. Brody turned on the radio. 'Hooper, he can't hear me. Can you tell him to come in?'

'OK,' said Hooper. 'I'll be there in a minute.'

The boat moved towards the boy. Below the water the shark felt something move in the sea. It turned and followed the boat.

The boy stopped swimming. He looked back to the shore. Brody called, 'Come in!' Now the boy heard him and he began to swim for the shore.

Hooper followed the boy. The boy looked back. 'What's wrong?' he said.

'Nothing,' said Hooper. 'Go back to the beach.'

The boy swam for twenty metres and then stood up in the water. He began to walk towards the shore.

Suddenly Hooper cried out, 'Shark! Get the boy out! Quick!'

The boy heard Hooper and tried to run. He fell into the water.

Brody ran into the water, but the sea pushed him back.

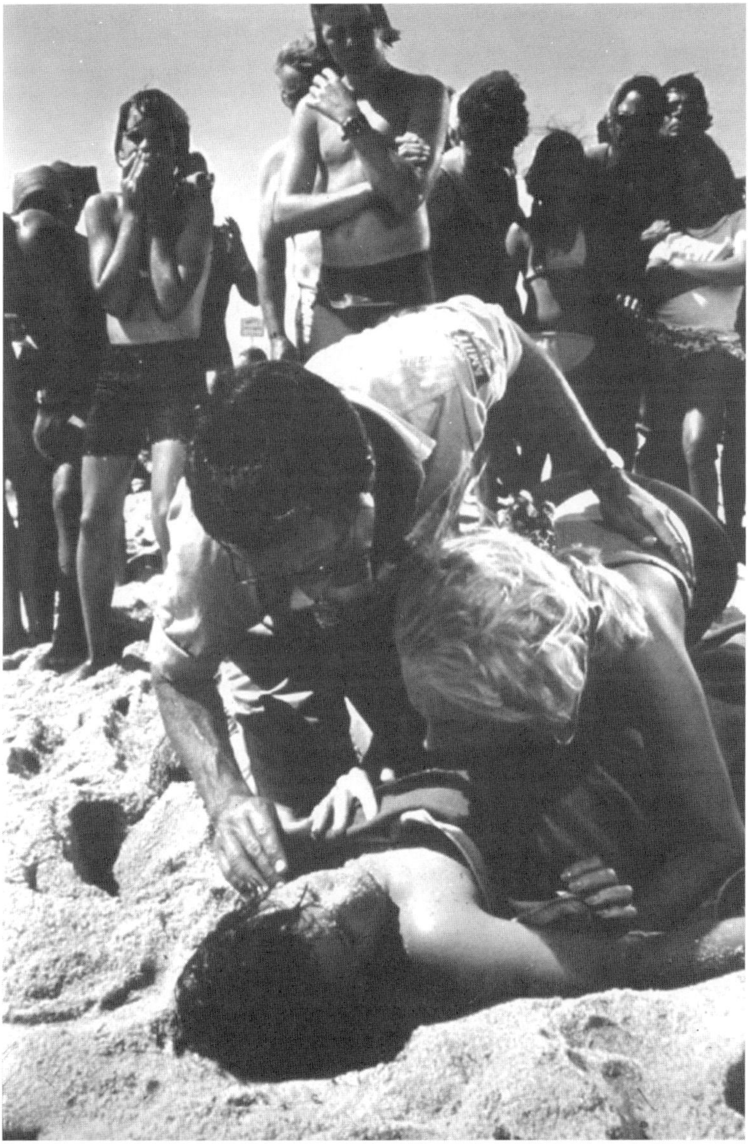

The boy lay on the beach. 'Are you OK?' Brody asked.

The boy moved fast now. He did not see the shark behind him.

'Quick!' said Brody. He ran into the water and pulled the boy out.

The shark went under again and swam away from the shore.

The boy lay on the beach. 'Are you OK?' Brody asked.

'I want to go home,' said the boy.

A man from the TV ran up to Brody and the boy. 'Can you do that again?' he said. 'We didn't get very good pictures.'

Brody was very angry. 'Go away!' he said. 'Everybody go home! I want nobody to go near the water. This beach is closed.'

Chapter 6 Quint

'What do you think, Harry?' said Brody. 'Can this man Quint help us?'

'We can try him,' said Meadows. 'We don't have anything to lose.'

'I don't think he can help,' said Hooper. 'This shark . . .'

'Do you have a better plan?' asked Brody. When Hooper did not answer, Brody picked up a phone book. 'Here it is. There's only one "Quint". And he doesn't have a first name.'

Brody phoned the number.

'Mr Quint, this is Martin Brody from Amity Police. We have a problem.'

'I know.'

'The shark was here again today.'

'Did it kill anybody?'

'No, but it nearly took a boy.'

'It's a big fish. It eats a lot of food.'

'Can you help us?' said Brody. 'This fish is killing people.'

'I'll try to kill it for you,' said Quint. 'But it'll be four hundred dollars a day.'

'That's a lot of money!' said Brody. 'There are other fishermen, you know.'

Quint laughed. 'Yes, you sent somebody out last week. And he's dead.'

'Can you start tomorrow?'

'I must have two men to help me.'

Brody did not want to help. He did not want to go in a boat again. But he said, 'I'll be there.'

Quint laughed again. 'Can you swim?'

'Yes. Why?'

'People sometimes fall overboard. And I want a second man.'

Brody turned to Hooper. 'Do you want to come?'

'Yes,' said Hooper. 'I want to see that fish.'

PART TWO

Chapter 7 Meat in the Water

They left at six in the morning. It was a very hot day and they sat out in the sun. Brody slept in a chair with a hat over his face. Hooper dropped food for the shark into the water. Quint sat next to a fishing line and watched the sea.

Suddenly Quint said, 'We've got a visitor.'

The three men stood up. 'Help me pull the line in,' said Quint.

They pulled the line out of the water. There was nothing on it. 'I think that was your friend,' said Quint. 'He broke our line.'

'What do we do now?' said Brody.

'We wait. Perhaps he'll take the other line.'

They waited. Nothing moved on the surface of the water. Then something pulled the second line.

They waited. Nothing moved on the surface of the water. Then something pulled the second line.

The line stopped moving.

'He did it again,' said Quint. 'We'll try a stronger line.'

Quint dropped a thicker line into the water. 'Come on!' he cried. 'I want to see you.'

'Will he break this line, too?' asked Brody.

'Yes, I think so,' said Quint. 'We can't stop him. I'm trying to bring him to the surface.'

The three men watched the line. Hooper dropped more meat into the water. Suddenly he saw something to his left. 'Look!' he cried.

The head of the shark was above the surface. It was three metres behind the boat and a metre out of the water. The three men saw its two black eyes and its half-open mouth. And they saw its teeth . . .

'Get a harpoon!' cried Quint.

He moved quickly to get the harpoon. At the same time the shark went back under the water.

'What a fish!' cried Hooper. 'His head was two metres across. How big was he?'

'It's hard to say,' said Quint. 'Perhaps eight metres. Perhaps more.'

'I hope he comes back!' said Hooper.

'Did he *smile* at us?' said Brody.

'No! His mouth was open,' said Quint. 'Remember, he's only a fish.'

'What do we do now?' asked Brody. 'Do we drop in more fish food for him?'

'No,' said Quint. 'We got him to the surface once. He'll be back.'

Suddenly a noise in the water made Hooper turn.

'Look,' said Quint.

The shark was ten metres from the boat.

'It's attacking the boat!' cried Brody.

'Hand me the harpoon,' said Quint.

The shark came very near. It looked at Hooper with one of its black eyes. Then it swam past below the boat. Quint picked up the harpoon.

'Behind you!' cried Hooper. 'He went under the boat.'

Quint turned and pointed the harpoon. The shark moved away from the boat and began to swim down. Quint sat down and laughed.

'That was lucky,' he said. 'He didn't attack the boat.' He looked at Brody. 'Are you OK?'

'I don't understand it,' said Brody. He thought about the young woman, Chrissie, and the boy, Alex Kintner. 'That thing isn't a fish.'

'It *is* a fish!' said Hooper. There was a smile on his face – he was very happy. 'And what a fish! It's beautiful!'

'Do you think he'll come back?' said Brody.

'I don't know,' said Quint. 'You never know what a shark is going to do.'

They waited for three hours, but the fish didn't come back. At five o'clock Quint said, 'Let's finish for today. I don't like to be out in this boat at night.'

Brody smiled. 'Yes, my wife doesn't like me to work at night!' he said.

'I don't have a wife,' said Quint.

Chapter 8 Black Eyes

'You're not putting that thing on my boat,' said Quint.

The boat was ready to go. Quint had his back to it. In front of him Brody and Hooper stood next to a big cage. The cage was over two metres tall and two metres across.

'Why not?' said Hooper.

'It's too big,' said Quint. 'What is it?'

'It's a shark-cage,' said Hooper. 'I want to go down into the water in it. I want to take some pictures of that fish.'

'No,' said Quint. 'Not on my boat.'

'Why not?'

'Because it's too dangerous. The fish will eat that cage for breakfast.'

'I don't think he will. And I want those pictures.'

'He says you can't,' said Brody. 'Forget it. We're going out there to kill that fish.'

'You can't stop me,' said Hooper.

'Oh yes, I can. The town of Amity is paying for this.'

Hooper said to Quint. 'I'll pay you.'

Quint smiled. 'How much?'

'I said no!' said Brody.

But Hooper did not listen to Brody. He said to Quint. 'A hundred dollars.'

Hooper gave Quint the money. Brody was very angry, but he did not want to lose more time. He said to Quint, 'Let's go.'

Quint took the boat out into the sea. Brody sat next to him. 'Are we going back to the same place?' he asked Quint.

'Yes. We'll be there soon.'

'Will the fish be there?'

'Who knows? But it's the only thing we can do. Sharks are not clever.'

Brody remembered the face of the shark. 'I don't know,' he said. 'That fish was clever yesterday.'

'No. He doesn't know what he's doing. Fish do different things sometimes. But I know everything they *can* do.'

'Can you catch every fish?'

'No. But not because they're clever. Sometimes they're not hungry. Or you can give them the wrong fish food.'

Quint was quiet for a time. Then he spoke again. 'Once,' he said, 'a shark nearly caught *me*. It was about twenty years ago. I had a blue shark on the line and he pulled me overboard with him.'

'What did you do?'

'I came up fast. I was lucky.'

Quint slowed the boat down. Suddenly it was quiet. 'OK, Hooper,' he said. 'Start throwing the fish food overboard.'

By ten o'clock there was a light wind. The men sat and watched the sea. They said nothing. Hooper dropped meat into the sea.

Brody got up to get a drink. Suddenly Quint said, 'There he is.'

Hooper jumped up and said, 'Yes! There he is!'

'Where?' said Brody.

'There,' said Quint. 'Behind you.'

Brody looked out to sea. The shark was forty metres away. 'What are we going to do?'

'Nothing,' said Quint. 'We'll wait. Hooper, drop more fish food in the sea. Let's bring him in here.'

Quint picked up a harpoon. The fish swam round the boat. Then it moved nearer.

'Come here, fish,' said Quint. 'Come here.'

But the fish did not come nearer.

'I don't understand,' said Quint. 'Throw some food into the water. And throw some bottles, too.'

'Why bottles?' asked Brody.

'Perhaps he'll swim towards them. We want him to come nearer.'

They threw things into the water. The shark moved nearer. Ten metres from the boat it stopped. Suddenly its head came up above the surface.

'Fish!' Quint called. 'Come here. We've got something for you!'

For a short time the shark watched them with its black eyes. Then its head went back below the water.

'Where did he go?' said Brody.

'I think he's coming now,' said Quint. 'Come on, fish!' he said. 'Come and get your dinner!' He pointed the harpoon down at the water.

Suddenly the boat moved below them. The three men fell over.

They got up and looked overboard. But there was nothing there.

'Where is he now?' said Brody.

'I don't know,' said Quint. 'But he'll come back.'

'Let's put the cage overboard,' said Hooper.

'No!' said Brody.

'It might bring him out. And I won't go down in it,' said Hooper. 'What do you say, Quint?'

'OK,' said Quint. 'You paid for it.' He put down the harpoon, and he and Hooper pushed the cage overboard. The three men looked into the water.

'Do you think the fish will come up?' said Brody.

'I think he'll come and look at the cage,' said Hooper.

Quint and Hooper pushed the cage overboard.

But the shark did not come up. After fifteen minutes, Hooper said, 'I'm going down there. Perhaps that'll bring him up.'

'Wait for the fish,' said Quint. 'He'll come up.'

'I don't want to wait ten years for him, Quint! I don't think you understand this fish.'

Quint looked at Hooper. 'Are you saying I don't know my job?'

'No. But I think I can kill the fish.'

'OK. Go and do it then.'

Brody said, 'We can't let him go down in that thing.'

But Quint did not listen. 'Go on,' he said to Hooper. 'Get in the cage.'

Hooper got into the cage and they dropped it overboard. It stopped two metres below the surface.

Quint picked up the harpoon.

'Will he be OK?' said Brody.

'I don't think he'll live for ten minutes down there.'

'Perhaps you're right. But you never know what these fish will do.'

'I know, but this is different. This is like putting your hand into a fire.'

Chapter 9 Cage

Below the surface Hooper looked for the shark. He knew that Quint was wrong. The shark was not below the boat. It did not 'sit' in any one place. Sharks never stopped moving.

Hooper turned slowly in the cage. He looked but saw nothing. A small fish swam towards his face. He pushed it out of the cage.

He looked down and started to look away. Then suddenly he saw something. The shark swam slowly towards him. Hooper watched it. What a beautiful fish!

It came nearer, and Hooper moved back. The shark's head was

now only about a metre from the cage. It turned and began to swim in front of Hooper's eyes.

Hooper put his hand out and touched it. It felt cold and hard.

The shark began to move away from the cage.

'What's he doing down there?' Brody asked.

Quint did not answer. He stood with his harpoon in his hand. He looked down at the water. 'Come up, fish,' he said. 'Come to Quint.'

'Do you see it?' said Brody. 'What's it doing?'

'Nothing.'

Hooper began taking photographs. He watched the shark turn towards him. It moved fast with its mouth open. He waited for the shark to turn again.

But the shark did not turn. It hit the cage and made a hole in it. Hooper fell back.

The shark did not turn. It hit the cage and made a hole in it. Hooper fell back.

'It's attacking!' cried Brody. He tried to pull the cage out of the water. 'Throw the harpoon!'

'I can't throw it! I must get him to the surface first. Come up! Come up!'

The shark moved back out of the cage. Hooper tried to get to the surface. He saw the hole in the cage.

The shark pushed its head through the hole again. Hooper moved to the back of the cage. The shark pushed again, and Hooper saw its teeth.

The jaws of the shark closed around him. Hooper pushed his hand into the black eye and thought 'I'm going to die . . .'

'He's got him!' cried Brody. 'Do something!'

'The man is dead,' Quint said.

'How do you know?'

'He's dead.'

The shark left the cage, and dropped down a metre. Then it swam up towards the surface.

'He's coming up!' said Brody.

The shark hit the surface five metres from the boat. It carried Hooper in its mouth. Quint threw the harpoon. But the shark began to swim down into the water, and the harpoon went over it. The shark dropped below the surface.

'What do we do now?' said Brody.

'We'll go back,' said Quint. 'For now.'

'But why do you want to come back? That fish is too strong for us!'

'I'm going to kill that thing,' said Quint.

'I don't think I can get more money for you.'

'This is not about money.'

'What are you saying?' Brody looked at Quint.

'I'm going to kill that fish. Do you want to come with me?'

Brody looked into Quint's eyes. They were as dark as the eyes of the shark. 'I'll come,' said Brody.

♦

Brody arrived home late that night. He told Ellen about Hooper. She was very sad.

'It's over now,' she said.

Brody did not answer for a time. Then he said, 'We're going out tomorrow. At six o'clock.'

'Why?' cried Ellen. 'What can you do?'

'We're going to catch the fish, and kill it.'

'Do you think you can?'

'I don't know. But Quint thinks we can. And it's my job to help him.'

'But it's *not* your job!' She was very angry and very afraid. She began to cry.

Brody said nothing. Then he said, 'No, you're right.'

'Then *why*?'

'I don't think I can tell you,' said Brody. 'I don't think I know.'

Chapter 10 Fight to the Finish

The next morning it rained. Brody met Quint at the boat.

'Is it only me and you this time?' said Brody.

'Yes,' said Quint. 'You know the fish as well as any man. Nobody can help us now.'

Quint turned the boat out to sea. After ten minutes he slowed it down. Brody looked back towards the shore. 'We're not out as far today,' he said. 'We can't be more than three kilometres from the shore.'

'That's right.'

'So why are you stopping?'

Quint pointed to the shore. 'I don't think he'll go out far today,' he said. 'I think he'll be somewhere between here and Amity.'

Quint stopped the boat and Brody began dropping meat into the sea. Quint threw a line overboard. Then he put a barrel on a harpoon line.

'OK,' said Quint. 'Now we wait.'

An hour went by. Nothing happened. Brody stood up and looked overboard.

Suddenly he saw the head of the shark, with its black eyes and open jaws. It was less than two metres away! 'Oh no!' Brody said. 'He's here!'

Quint jumped up. The shark's head dropped back into the water. A minute later it hit the boat. The boat moved up and down. Then the shark went under again and the boat stopped moving.

'He waited for us!' cried Brody. 'How did he . . . ?'

'I don't know,' said Quint. 'We've got him now.'

'*We've* got *him*? Did you see what he did to the boat? He's got *us*, I say!'

The line moved, and there were noises from under the boat.

Quint stood and picked up a harpoon-gun. 'He'll be back soon.'

The boat moved again.

Quint put his head overboard, and cried, 'Come out from under there!'

'What's he doing?' Brody asked.

'He's making a hole in the boat. Look, the water's coming in . . . Come out and I'll kill you!'

The shark came to the surface, and began to move towards the boat.

'Come to me,' said Quint. 'Come to me.' He stood and watched the shark. When it was a metre from the boat, he used the gun.

The harpoon hit the shark. And then the shark hit the boat, hard. Quint fell back and his head hit a chair. He jumped to his feet again and cried, 'I got you!'

The harpoon line went overboard. It pulled the barrel into the water with it.

He stood and watched the shark. When it was a metre from the boat, he used the gun.

'He took it down with him!' said Brody.

'Not for long,' said Quint. 'He'll be back! When he comes, we'll throw harpoons at him again and again and again. And then we'll have him!'

Quint watched the water. 'Get another barrel,' he said. 'Bring it back here.'

Brody ran to the front of the boat and got a barrel. He carried it over to Quint.

'Here he comes!' said Quint. He pointed down to the left. The barrel came to the surface and moved in the water. Quint picked up a harpoon. 'He's coming up!'

The shark jumped out of the water. It was less than three metres from the boat.

'I'll get you!' cried Quint, and he threw the second harpoon. The harpoon hit the shark and it fell back into the sea. Water came over the boat.

The second line went overboard. 'We've got him!' said Quint.

The boat moved once and then again. They heard the sound of something breaking.

'Do you want to attack again?' said Quint. 'You won't take any man with you!'

Quint started the boat, and they began moving away.

'Is the boat OK?' said Brody.

'He made a hole under us,' said Quint. 'But we'll be OK.'

'That's it then,' Brody said happily. 'The fish is dead.'

'No,' said Quint. 'Look.'

Brody looked back and saw the two red barrels in the sea behind them.

'Why is he coming after us? Does he think we're food?'

'No. He wants to fight us.'

For the first time, Quint was afraid.

'Do sharks usually do this?'

'No,' said Quint. 'They sometimes attack the boat. But they stop after you hit them with a harpoon. But this one wants to fight. So we'll fight him!'

Quint drove the boat faster. The barrels came after them. He slowed the boat and picked up a third harpoon. 'OK!' he called. 'Come and get it!'

The barrels came through the water. They were forty metres away, then thirty, then twenty. Brody saw the shark swim past the boat below the water. It was two metres from the surface. 'He's here!' he cried.

The shark swam past the boat. After forty metres it turned. Its head came out of the water, and then dropped back in. 'Here he comes!' said Quint.

The shark hit the boat and Quint threw his harpoon. It hit the shark in the head, over the right eye. The line went slowly overboard.

'I got him in the head!' said Quint.

But the barrels moved on across the surface of the water. Then they went under.

'What's he *doing*?' said Quint. 'No fish can attack with three harpoons in him! But he can't live for much longer. And we can wait!'

For three hours they waited. They watched the barrels move slowly across the surface of the sea.

At eleven o'clock the rain stopped. Then for nearly an hour the barrels did not move.

'What do you think?' said Brody. 'Is he dead?'

'I don't think so. But perhaps we can pull him in with a strong line.'

They began to pull him in. The shark was very heavy. The barrels did not move.

Then suddenly the line started coming at them fast.

'Did the line break?' said Brody.

'No!' said Quint. Brody saw he was afraid. 'He's coming up.'

Quint started the boat. But it was too late.

The shark came up above the surface. Brody watched it jump, and cried out.

The shark dropped down on to the back of the boat, and pushed it below the surface. The water came up their legs.

The shark was now only a metre from Brody's head. He looked into its big black eye and thought, 'I'm going to die . . .'

'Look what you did to my boat!' cried Quint. He picked up a harpoon and pushed it hard into the shark's head.

The boat started going down. The shark fell back into the sea, but the line from the harpoon began pulling Quint into the water.

Brody tried to help him, but it was too late. The big fisherman went slowly down, under the dark water.

The shark slowly fell back below the surface of the water, down and down, out of the light.

For a short time there was no sound. The water was up to Brody's mouth now. Twenty metres away the shark came back up above the surface. 'Go away!' cried Brody.

The big fish came nearer and nearer. Brody cried out. Then he closed his eyes and waited.

Nothing happened. When Brody opened his eyes he saw the shark there next to him. For a short time it did not move. Then it slowly fell back below the surface of the water, down and down, out of the light. It pulled Quint's body behind it.

Brody watched the dead shark fall down and down into the sea. Then he began to swim towards the shore.

ACTIVITIES

Chapters 1–2

Before you read

1 Do you know the story of *Jaws*? Did you see the film? Talk to other students.

2 Look at the Word List at the back of the book. Finish these sentences.

The old (a)... often goes in his boat. He puts a small fish on the end of a (b)... and waits. He catches a lot of fish and puts them in a (c)... . One day a very big (d)... swam near the boat. It came up to the (e)... but then it swam down and away. The fisherman was happy when he got back to the (f)... that day.

3 Read the Introduction to the story. Which are the right words in *italics* in these sentences?

- **a** This story happens in a *small town / big city*.
- **b** A shark attacks a *policeman / young woman*.
- **c** The *Amity police / important people* want to close the beaches.

While you read

4 Who ...

- **a** does the shark kill? ....
- **b** falls asleep on the beach? ....
- **c** finds a woman's head on the beach? ....
- **d** knows a lot about sharks? ....
- **e** won't write the story for the town newspaper? ....
- **f** is a rich and important man in Amity? ....

After you read

5 Work with another student. Have this conversation.

Student A: You are Martin Brody. You want to close the beaches.

Student B: You are Larry Vaughan. You don't want to close the beaches.

Chapters 3–4

Before you read

6 The beaches are staying open and the summer visitors will come. What do you think will happen?

While you read

7 Read these sentences about Chapter 3. Are they right (✓) or wrong (✗)?

- **a** The people on the beach know about the shark attacks. .....
- **b** The boy's mother says he can go out in his boat. .....
- **c** The shark sees the boy and his boat in the sea. .....
- **d** A man on the beach sees the shark. .....
- **e** On Monday there are stories about Amity in the newspapers. .....
- **f** The boy's mother reads the newspapers. 'You killed Alex!' she tells Brody. .....

8 Which of these things happen in Chapter 4? Tick (✓) the boxes.

- **a** Ben Gardner calls his wife on his radio. [__]
- **b** When Brody and Hendricks get to the *Flicka*, they find Ben. [__]
- **c** Ben's radio makes a sudden noise. [__]
- **d** Hendricks finds a shark's tooth in the boat. [__]
- **e** Hooper says the tooth is from a very big Great White Shark. [__]

9 Matt Hooper knows a lot about sharks. Which of these words does he use about the shark?

very big ..... clever .....

thinks a lot ..... afraid of nothing .....

After you read

10 Work with a friend. Ask and answer about the shark attack.

Student A: You are a newspaper man from New York City.

Student B: You were in the sea when the shark attacked the boy.

11 Look at the photograph on page 13. Answer these questions.

a Who are the three men and what are they talking about?

b There is a big picture behind the men. Somebody changed the picture with a black pen. How?

Chapters 5–6

Before you read

12 Do you think Brody will open the beaches again before they catch the shark?

13 Who will go in the boat, do you think?

While you read

14 Find the mistakes in these sentences. Underline the wrong words. Write the right words.

a Larry Vaughan, Harry Meadows and Matt Hooper want to close the beaches. ....

b The people on the beaches aren't thinking about the shark. ....

c Brody is out in Ben Gardner's boat. ....

d Hooper and the boy talk by radio. ....

e The shark catches the boy. ....

f The TV people get good pictures of the boy and the shark. ....

g Quint doesn't know about Amity's problem with the shark. ....

h Brody loves boats. ....

After you read

15 Answer the questions.

a On Sunday night, Matt Hooper says to Martin Brody, 'I don't think the shark is here.' Why does he think this?

b Brody says he will open the beaches. What will Hooper do when they are open?

c Why does Brody say to the boy, 'Come in'?

d Why is Brody angry with the TV man?

e Why does Brody say he will go in the boat?

f Why does Quint say he wants another man?

16 Who do you want to win – the town or the shark? Why?

Chapters 7–8

Before you read

17 They are going to try to kill the shark. What do you think they will take with them in the boat?

18 You are Brody. Will you go in the boat? Or will you stay on the shore and use your radio?

While you read

19 Here are Brody's notes for Day 1. Finish the notes.

a We leave the shore at ....

b The shark breaks .... lines.

c We see the shark .... times.

d We go back to the shore at ....

20 Which of these things do they throw into the water on Day 2?

some meat .....   some bottles .....

the harpoon .....   the cage .....

After you read

21 Make sentences about the shark with these words.

a black   **b** two metres   **c** eight metres

22 What do you think of Brody, Hooper and Quint? Think of two words for each man. Use your dictionary.

Chapters 9–10

Before you read

23 Will more people die before the end of the story?

24 Who will win – the shark or the men?

While you read

25 Put these words in the sentences.

cage doesn't eye hand harpoon Hooper photographs shark

a Hooper puts his .... on the shark.

b Hooper wants .... of the shark.

c Matt thinks the shark will turn away from the ....

d The shark .... turn away from the cage.

e The .... makes a hole in the cage.

f Hooper pushes his hand into the shark's ....

g The shark comes up to the surface with .... in its mouth.

h Quint throws a .... but it doesn't hit the shark.

26 Write *B* for Brody or *Q* for Quint.

a He stops the boat three kilometres from the shore. .....

b He suddenly sees the shark two metres away. .....

c He hits his head on a chair. .....

d He says the shark wants to fight them. .....

e He starts the boat but they can't get away. .....

f He sees the shark's eye and thinks he's going to die. .....

g The shark pulls him into the sea. .....

h He swims back to the shore. .....

After you read

27 How many harpoons hit the shark? .....

28 Why are these things important at the end of the story?

the cage   meat   harpoons   barrels

29 How many people does the shark kill in this story? Write the names.

30 The shark is dead. Two friends from Amity stand on Old Mill Beach and look at the sea. Have this conversation.

Student A: You want to go for a swim.

Student B: You don't want to go for a swim.

Writing

31 Find out about sharks. Where do they live? How many different sharks are there? How many shark attacks are there each year? How important are they in the life of the sea? Write about them.

32 You work for a holiday company in Amity. You want visitors to come back to Amity after the shark problems. Write about the beaches, the town, the people, the weather, the hotels ...

33 You are Mrs Kintner. Write a letter to Brody's boss. Say that you are angry with Brody.

34 You are Brody's wife Ellen. She writes to her sister and tells her about the last week in Amity. She tells her sister about Martin. He feels bad about Alex, the old man, Ben, Matt Hooper and Quint.

35 What animals are you afraid of? Why do you feel afraid? Write about them.

36 The fight at the end is between Quint and the shark. The shark is not interested in Brody. How does Quint feel about the shark? How does the shark feel about Quint? Write about it.

37 Larry Vaughan calls all the people in Amity to the town square. He tells them about Matt Hooper and Quint. He says thank you to Brody. He names the dead people. He says he is sorry. Write his words.

38 Write about one of the photographs in the book. What is happening? What happened before? What is going to happen next? Why is this important in the story?

Answers for the Activities in this book are available from the Penguin Readers website. A free Activity Worksheet is also available from the website. Activity Worksheets are part of the Penguin Teacher Support Programme, which also includes Progress Tests and Graded Reader Guidelines. For more information, please visit: www.penguinreaders.com.

WORD LIST *with example sentences*

attack (v/n) Some animals are dangerous and can *attack* people.
barrel (n) They threw all the dead fish into an old *barrel*.
body (n) There was a dead *body* in the water. It was the *body* of a man.
cage (n) Some people have a bird in a *cage* at home.
drop (v) I *dropped* some food into the water, and the fish came for it.
far (adj/adv) The shop is not *far* from here – only about 200 metres.
fisherman (n) This *fisherman* caught a very big fish yesterday.
harpoon (n) The long *harpoon* flew from the harpoon-gun into the big fish.
hole (n) The water came in through a *hole* in the boat.
jaw (n) The big teeth in its strong *jaws* are very dangerous.
line (n) There was a big fish at the other end of my fishing *line*.
must (v) This animal is very dangerous. We *must* kill it.
overboard (adv) A girl on the boat fell *overboard*. She could swim so she was OK.
pick up (v) His hat was on the beach. He *picked* it *up* and carried it.
point (v) 'Look!' said the man, and he *pointed* at the big fish.
shark (n) *Sharks* don't often kill people in the sea.
shore (n) We swam to the *shore* and then sat on the beach.
slow (v) The boat *slowed* and then stopped.
surface (n) The fish came up to the *surface* and then went down again.
towards (prep) A car came *towards* him but stopped five metres away.

Treasure Island

Robert Louis Stevenson

Young Jim Hawkins lives quietly by the sea with his mother and father. One day, Billy Bones comes to live with them and everything changes. Jim meets Long John Silver and they travel the seas to find Treasure Island.

The Mummy

"Imhotep is half-dead and will be half-dead for all time."

The Mummy is an exciting movie. Imhotep dies in Ancient Egypt. 3,700 years later Rick O'Connell finds him. Imhotep is very dangerous. Can O'Connell send him back to the dead? *Based on the successful film.*

Pirates of the Caribbean

The Curse of the Black Pearl

Elizabeth lives on a Caribbean island, a very dangerous place. A young blacksmith is interested in her, but pirates are interested too. Where do the pirates come from and what do they want? Is there really a curse on their ship? And why can't they enjoy their gold?

There are hundreds of Penguin Readers to choose from – world classics, film adaptations, modern-day crime and adventure, short stories, biographies, American classics, non-fiction, plays ...

For a complete list of all Penguin Readers titles, please contact your local Pearson Longman office or visit our website.

www.penguinreaders.com